Finding the Language

Published and distributed by:
Voices of Future Generations International Children's Book Series
www.vofg.org

Edited by Allison Lalla, Sarah Sanders and Odeeth Lara
Layout: Steiner Graphics

The Voices of Future Generations International Children's Book Series:
'The Tree of Hope' by Kehkashan Basu (Middle East), illustrated by Karen Webb-Meek
'The Epic Eco-Inventions' by Jona David (Europe/North America), illustrated by Carol Adlam 'The Fireflies
After the Typhoon' by Anna Kuo (Asia), illustrated by Siri Vinter
'The Forward and Backward City' by Diwa Boateng (Africa), illustrated by Meryl Treatner
'The Sisters' Mind Connection' by Allison Lievano-Gomez (Latin America), illustrated by Oscar Pinto
'The Voice of an Island' by Lupe Vaai (Pacific Islands), illustrated by Li-Wen Chu
'The Visible Girls' by Tyronah Sioni (Pacific Islands), illustrated by Kasia Nieżywińska
'The Great Green Vine Invention' by Jona David (Europe/North America), illustrated by Carol Adlam
'The Mechanical Chess Invention' by Jona David (Europe/North America), illustrated by Dan Ungureanu
'A Path to Life' by Ying-Xuan Lai (Asia), illustrated by Kasia Nieżywińska
'The Cosmic Climate Invention' by Jona David (Europe/North America), illustrated by Dan Ungureanu
'The Sound of Silence' by Ying-Xuan Lai (Asia), illustrated by Kasia Nieżywińska
'The White Dolphin' by Zhuo Meng-Xin (Asia), illustrated by Li-Wen Chu
'The Small Sparrow Hero' by Huang Yun-Hung (Asia), illustrated by Celia Tian
'Journey for Tomorrow' by Andrea Wilson (North America) illustrated by Vikki Zhang
'The Children Who Saved the Mangroves' by Rehema Kubigi (Africa), illustrated by Justine Greenfield
'Stanley and EPIC' by Jasper Chin Moody (Oceania), illustrated by Celia Tian
'Dream Catcher' by Tien-Li Cheng (Asia), illustrated by Dianne Green
'Finding the Language' by Adelyn Newman-Ting (Indigenous), illustrated by Justine Greenfield
'The Girl Who Changed Everything' (Europe), illustrated by Li-Wen Chu

Voices of Future Generations Children's Book Series

Under the patronage of
UNESCO
United Nations
Educational, Scientific and
Cultural Organization

United Nations
Educational, Scientific and
Cultural Organization

Canadian Commission for UNESCO

CISDL
Centre for International
Sustainable Development Law

World Future Council

Fundación ECOS

WORLD'S LARGEST LESSON

OMBUDSMAN FOR FUTURE GENERATIONS

環境品質文教基金會
Environmental Quality Protection Foundation

MOORE CHARITABLE FOUNDATION

This book is printed on recycled paper, using sustainable and low-carbon printing methods.

Finding the Language

by

Adelyn Newman-Ting

Illustrated by Justine Greenfield

foreword

In this beautifully written story by Adelyn Newman-Ting, we are introduced to Kesugilakw (Kesu) and Bob, who have been friends since they were babies. One day they head out to the forest to play and find themselves in a mysterious place.

It is in this place that they meet gwa'wina, a raven, and a wolf named u'ligaan, both of whom can talk and who can understand Kesu and Bob. The animals explain to the two children how the land created Indigenous languages and how both the land and Indigenous languages are at risk.

The four of them become fast friends and develop a plan to raise awareness with other children in the community about the risk to the land and languages. They bring all the children together and share information about UNESCO and the Sustainable Development Goals, specifically Goals 4 and 13. Goal 4 seeks to ensure inclusive and equitable high-quality education and promote lifelong learning opportunities for all, and SDG 13 asks us all to take urgent action to combat climate change and its impacts. Adelyn brilliantly weaves in the importance of the United Nations Declaration on the Rights of Indigenous People. She helps the reader understand the beauty and importance of languages by infusing Kwakwala throughout the story.

As the children set out to save the land and languages, they meet various Elders who share wisdom and cultural teachings that help guide them in a good way.

An epic adventure unfolds and provides the reader with insight into how both animals and humans can care for the land and support the continued revitalization of Indigenous languages. It is a story about reverence for the land, the water and Indigenous languages. It is about friendships and the importance of caring for each other, and ultimately about love.

I look forward to reading the next adventure Adelyn writes.

— *Ms. Monique Gray Smith*
Cree, Lakota and Scottish award-winning and best-selling author

preface

Gilakas'la! You may have heard the phrase "All my relations" uttered at the end of a speech, ceremony or prayer. In many Indigenous languages there is a word or a phrase that means much the same thing. In Kwak'wala we say namwayut, which means we are all one. We humans are one with the trees, the plants, the four-legged and winged, the winds, the waters, the earth. When we remember this, we know that when we take care of the earth, we are actually taking care of ourselves too because we are part of the earth. We have been taught to forget this important truth and to imagine that we humans could fly off to another planet when we have worn this one out. Thinking that we can control everything and that the earth will just continue to create resources that we extract and turn into profit is dangerous and robs our youth of their future.

Our niece Kesugwilakw - Ting Li-We - Adelyn's generation has a tremendous task trying to turn adult attention to caring for ourselves and the environment. They are going to need help with this until they are the leaders who make the decisions. We proud aunties are here to lend our hearts, minds and hands to the task ahead. We promise to continue listening to and learning the language and ways of the land we walk on, in cities and in forests, and the waters we drink, travel on and fish from. Most of all we will continue to listen to and act upon the wisdom of our young ones who share their knowledge, hope and understanding of how we will work together to give the earth, and therefore ourselves, a better chance. He'mass. That is everything.

With all of our love,

Kugwi' sila' ogwa - proud Auntie Ellen
&
Nega' ga - proud Auntie Marion

'Namba 1

This is the story of two friends, Kesugilakw and Bob, who came together with their animal friends to help save the environment and Indigenous languages at the same time. Kesugilakw, who goes by the nickname Kesu, has long brown hair the colour of the forest floor, dark brown eyes like the colour of an oak leaf in fall, and skin the color of honey. Bob has reddish-orange hair, like the last colour a maple leaf turns before it falls from a tree, blue eyes like the colour of the sky at daytime, and freckles. They have been good friends for a long time, and both care deeply about animals and the environment.

One day, Kesu and Bob, who were having a sleepover, woke up in Kesu's very old, wooden house that had been painted with Kwakwaka'wakw native designs by Kesu's great-great-grandfather. Her father had always wanted to go over the old faded paint with new paint, but he'd never found the time.

Kesu lived with her parents and grandparents in a large house in a medium-sized town that was filled with a bunch of big totem poles. The town was surrounded by the forest and ocean, quite far away from the closest big city.

The children headed downstairs for breakfast. They had been up late playing and having a party where no adults were allowed. When they got to the kitchen, they asked Kesu's parents if they could go and play in the forest after they ate. Kesu's mom said that they could, so they gobbled up their breakfasts like bears waking from hibernation. Then they got their coats and shoes on and ran out the door and into the forest.

They tromped through the forest as loud as a pack of wolves.
Eventually, they came across something mysterious that they
had never seen before. It looked as if someone or something
had created a secret place out of branches and trees. Curious,
they parted the branches and went inside.

Ma'łba 2

Once inside the secret location, Kesu and Bob stood there for a few minutes, amazed by what they saw in front of them. They were standing in a giant ring. The ground was a mossy mixture of greens with a sprinkle of light brown color. The trees that made the walls of the ring were very tall, with bark like melted dark chocolate. The leaves, needles and boughs up above looked like emeralds and shimmered in the sunlight. In one area, there were five little stumps covered in leaves, like stools with leafy cushions. They were arranged around a bigger stump that was like a table made by nature. The children decided to sit down and think for a few minutes.

Just as they sat down, two animals appeared through the leafy circle of trees. The animals came and joined them at the table. "Hi," said u'ligan, a wolf cub.

"Who are you?" asked gwa'wina, a young raven.

The children were speechless. Could they actually understand what these animals were saying?

"Oh my!" exclaimed Bob, bewildered as to what was happening.

"We are children from the village not too far away," said Kesugilakw, who was less surprised because she had always heard stories from her grandparents of animals that could talk. Still, when she had run into the forest a few minutes ago, this was not what she had expected to be doing.

Yudaxw ³

"Welcome to our house. But what are you doing here?" asked gwa'wina and u'ligan together. They were curious because humans rarely visited them.

"We are friends, I'm Kesu and this is Bob," Kesu began to explain excitedly. "We came out today to play in the forest but saw the entrance to somewhere we had never seen before and thought it would be fun to check it out. I promise we mean you no harm! My grandmother always tells me stories about animals who can talk to people and that we need to respect all animals," she added in case the animals were afraid.

"Very nice to meet you, Kesu and Bob," gwa'wina said kindly. "I'm gwa'wina and this is u'ligan. Like you, we are very good friends! You see, ravens are creative, fun-loving tricksters and wolves are natural teachers and pathfinders. In nature, our species often travel together. We have been friends ever since we were a hatchling and a cub!"

"We have been best friends since we were babies too! In fact, our parents met at a parenting class before we were born, and we have been best friends ever since," Kesu added.

Still bewildered, Bob asked "How can we all understand each other here when I can't understand the animals at home?"

"That's a good question," said Kesu, trying to remember what her grandmother had told her.

"It's because this land is magical," said u'ligan. "People and animals have been taking care of it together for a long time."

"But there are less and less people speaking Kwakwala, the traditional language of these lands. The land has invented language over time, and as humans came along, they found the words by the ocean, under rocks, deep, deep in the forests and sometimes in caves," gwa'wina continued.

"And if we don't take care of the lands then we will lose the languages too. The lands and water are getting polluted by gasoline and rubbish. Forests are being logged in cruel ways. When all of the trees are cut down in one area, it brings sadness like a storm that would never end," u'ligan explained sadly.

"But this can't happen!" Kesu and Bob cried out together.

Mu 4

After realizing that they all had the same ideas, the children and the animals decided that they would start working together to do something to save the land and the language.

"If you let us stay for a little bit, then we will do something together that you can't do alone. We will help you save the language, both for your sake and ours," said Kesu thoughtfully.

"We have been wanting to revitalize the language for a long time. If you could help us do that, we would be grateful, and you could visit here as much as you want, of course," said gwa'wina and u'ligan.

"So, I guess that brings us to our first step of the project," said Kesu.

gwa'wina and u'ligan started asking the kids questions about how they could bring their project to life.

"Should we ask other people to join?" asked u'ligan.

"How will we notify other people?" asked gwa'wina. "And what if other people reveal our secret place?"

"In response to your first question, yes we should ask a few other people to join," said Kesu. "Maybe gwa'wina can fly around from village to village and transform into a human to tell other villages, towns and cities about our plan. Also, gwa'wina can drop notes asking kids to please come and help save our languages."

"Maybe we should meet at Kesu's house and make everyone promise not to tell about the clubhouse before we show it to them," Bob suggested cautiously, wanting to protect the forest and his new friends.

"I will gladly fly from village to village delivering the message about the club and the instruction to meet at Kesu's house if they would like to join," gwa'wina said eagerly.

"What can I do?" asked u'ligan.

"You can go and get other wolves to help find the elders," suggested Kesu. "The elders can help us to understand the language."

A couple of days later, children started coming to Kesu's house by following the maps that gwa'wina left in each town. Meanwhile, u'ligan and the other wolves were guiding an elder to the clubhouse where they met up with gwa'wina and waited for Kesu and Bob to arrive with all the children.

All of the children had received the message and were coming because they wanted to help. Kesu and Bob were waiting in front of Kesu's house with a signup sheet asking some very important questions:

Do you want to save the land?
Do you know about UNESCO SDGs 4 and 13?
Do you want to revitalize the language?
Do you know about UNDRIP article 13?
Do you promise not to tell about the clubhouse if we show you?

As the children filled out these forms they started to talk excitedly about their answers. A couple of kids hadn't learned about the SDGs, so Bob explained: "SDG stands for Sustainable Development Goal, and UNESCO stands for United Nations Educational, Scientific, and Cultural Organization."

"SDG 4 is to ensure inclusive and equitable quality education and promote lifelong learning opportunities for all, and SDG 13 asks us all to take urgent action to combat climate change and its impacts."

"Okay, so what is UNDRIP?" asked another.

"UNDRIP stands for United Nations Declaration on the Rights of Indigenous Peoples and article 13 is the right to language." said Bob.

Once all of the kids had handed in their forms, Kesu and Bob gave them name tags for their shirts and jackets and then took them to the secret clubhouse where gwa'wina and u'ligan greeted them happily.

Saka 5

The elder, a friendly looking woman wearing a bright pink sweatsuit and glasses, approached Kesu and gave her a very special woven cedar bracelet that shimmered like polished copper and whispered to her, "In our language we call this kukwala. It is a bracelet that contains something that you might need on your journey, but for now, only you can know, so don't tell anyone else.

You will know when the time comes to tell the others."

Turning to the group of children, the elder announced: "Now I will give you the first clue. I can't teach you the full language, because I didn't learn it all when I was a child. It is up to you, the youth, to retrace the steps of our culture and retrieve our language. I will tell you this first clue in English, using a couple of Kwakwala words, and it will lead you to the next few words of Kesu's traditional language."

Clue #1: "u'ligan will guide you through the forest on a trail that is known only by wolves. Look for the path where the kadzakw roses grow, and there you will find your next clue."

One of the other children, a quiet boy with brown hair and brown eyes wearing a blue t-shirt and neon green shorts named Ash spoke up. "I think I know what that word means," he said, "my auntie made lots of them for a potlatch I went to last winter! They are roses made from cedar bark!" he exclaimed.

Kesu remembered a nearby forest where she helped to harvest cedar bark to be made into rope and hair for her father's carvings and told the others that it might be a good place to start looking for the next clue. "Some of us should stay here to figure out the Kwakwala clues, and the rest can come with Bob and me on the journey," Kesu explained. "gwa'wina, can you fly back and forth between the two teams so that the group at the clubhouse can quickly decode the clues as we collect them?" Everyone nodded in agreement.

Then u'ligan asked, "Who will go with you?"

"Well, it will depend." Kesu replied. "Would anyone like to stay to do the decoding?" she asked. Five kids quickly raised their hands. Kesu asked the others if they wanted to come and they nodded their heads enthusiastically, and then led by u'ligan, Kesu, Bob and the teammates left the secret clubhouse. The little group travelled along the path, two by two, setting off on a journey to find the second clue. Through the woods they padded, as quiet as mice. They travelled for a long while, and then paused for a brief moment for some water and snacks, which Bob had dutifully prepared in a little bag. Then they set off again.

Soon u'ligan spotted a tree with a long, narrow strip of bark peeled off, and shouted. "It's a culturally modified tree!" "This is the place where we peel cedar bark, there is only one strip missing because we only peel a little bit off so that the tree can keep growing" Kesu explained excitedly.

"I think that they are called 'culturally modified' because the bark is taken for cultural reasons." Ash explained.

"Is there something odd about this tree or is it just me?" questioned Bob.

"I noticed something too!" Kesu stated confidently.

"I think we should see what's on the other side!" exclaimed u'ligan.

"Okay," agreed Bob. They carefully parted the branches and stepped through to find a cedar rose workshop, and there in the middle of it all, an elder sat there working contentedly.

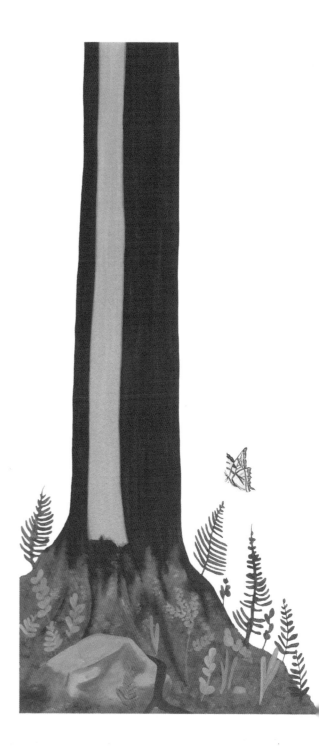

katła 6

"Hello children!" said the elder in a soft and pretty voice. She was wearing a long blue skirt, lilac shirt and white cardigan, and smiled knowingly, as if she had been expecting them.

"Oh, hi," giggled Kesu shyly.

"We are on a quest to bring back our language and we're told to come here. We are hoping that you might be able to give us the next clue!" stated Bob.

"What are your names?" questioned the elder. One by one, the children and animals said their names.

"Oh, how rude of me, I didn't even ask your name. What is your name?" questioned Kesu.

"Just call me łakwani," replied the elder. "It means old woman."

"Okay, no time to doddle, we must get moving with our goal!" exclaimed Kesu.

"Okay!" Everyone chorused at the same time.

"Remember the UNESCO SDGs?" asked Kesu.

"Yup!" Everyone chorused with enthusiasm.

"łakwani, please give us our next hint as to how to recover our language," one of the children asked sincerely.
Then the elder gave them the next clue:

Clue #2: "kadzatłege' to the mossy lagoon, and there you will find clue number three."

"Thank you!" exclaimed the children in unison.

"But what does kadzatłege' mean?" wondered Kesu out loud.
"How would you get to the lagoon?" łakwani replied, parting some branches to reveal a river nearby, glimmering and flowing smoothly.

"Walk along the river?" they asked. łakwani just nodded and smiled.

They all thanked her once again and set off following the river in search of a mossy lagoon. As they were leaving gwa'wina flew over and they gave gwa'wina the clue.

After they had walked for a few kilometers, U'ligan blurted out "There!" motioning to a grove so mossy that it almost hid a cave in the rocks. The group approached slowly and as they peered inside, they saw an elder whispering to the birds.

"Hi!" called Bob.

"Oh, hello" whispered the elder. He was wearing a dark green long-sleeved shirt and dark blue jeans.

Kesu touched her bracelet. "Sorry to interrupt, but we are looking for the next clue."

"Ah yes…" he replied thoughtfully.

Clue #3: Follow the brightest tutu and you will get the last clue and finish part one of the journey.

adłabu 7

"I think that tutu means star," said Kesu. "I remember because I always thought that it was funny that it was almost the same as the dress I wear for ballet!" gwa'wina flew in and they handed gwa'wina the clue.

It was just starting to get dark, and as children looked up into the sky, they spotted one star that was shining brighter than the others.

"I see it!" shouted Bob.

"Let's go!" declared Kesu.

They followed the star until they came to a very unusual structure. "Unusual indeed," Bob said. The structure was partly a treehouse hanging from the large tree above, and part house built on the ground with a branch poking out of a hole in the wall and a whole tree growing through the roof! There was a shelter off one side and a garage like thing off the other. THERE WAS EVEN A DECK ON THE ROOF! (Of the ground house of course). The wooden siding was painted light butter yellow and the shingles on the roof were so covered in moss you could barely see them. There were brightly colored wildflowers in white planter boxes and there was a flickering glow from the windows, like it was being lit by a fireplace or candles. But the thing that caught their attention the most was a glittering star hung above the door that they realized was the same as the star they were following. "A house and a treehouse in one!?"

blurted Bob. They went and knocked on the door and an elder came and opened the door. The elder was wearing a brightly coloured flower print shirt and beige shorts that were baggy and went down to his knees.

"Hi," whispered Kesu timidly, completely surprised by the elder's outfit (she was not used to elders wearing flower print or beige).

"Hello," said the elder cheerfully.

"We are here for the next clue!" everyone else chorused, completely unsurprised at the elder's clothing (Because their grandparents wore stuff like that all the time).

"Oh yes, yes, come in," the elder told the children.

"Come on," Kesu told everyone as they crowded in.

"So, I see you are here for the next clue," said the elder.

"Yes, we are," replied u'ligan.

"The clue here is only in Kwakwala. Do you still want it?" the elder said with an intense stare. "Of course, you do, I was only joking! To understand your final clue, you need to put together the Kwakwala words from some of the clues."

The children thought about the group back at the clubhouse and silently wished that they would be able to decipher the clues quickly. Sure enough, a few minutes later gwa'wina and the other kids came bursting through the trees. "We decoded the Kwakwala clues!" they announced.

"Hold on," said Kesu, "We still have one more to go."

"Oh," they said, clearly disappointed.

"We need to take the Kwakwala words from all the clues and put them together."

The elder took a look at the paper gwa'wina had in her beak. On it the kids had written the deciphered clues. "It says here kadzatłege', 'kadzakw and tutu. I have only one word to add and that word is *kukwala*" said the elder.

Clue #4: Three must stay and one must go.

"Well we know that kadzakw means cedar bark, and tutu means star," said one of the kids.

"We also know that kadzatłege' means to walk along the river," said another.

"But what does kukwala mean?" chorused the others.

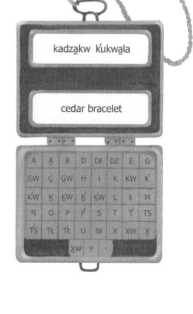

"I know!" Kesu exclaimed, "that was the word that the elder in the bright pink sweatsuit and glasses whispered to me. It means bracelet!"

"So, the last clue is walk along the river-bracelet-star-cedar bark?" asked Bob.

The children decided that of the four clues, the walk along the riverbank seemed like the one that had to go, but which star? What cedar bark? Whose bracelet? The children all wondered.

Everyone took a moment to think. Kesu looked down at her bracelet, noticing for the first time that her bracelet had a star on one of the beads. "My cedar bracelet!" Kesu burst out suddenly, pointing to the bracelet given to her by the first elder they had met. Everyone crowded around Kesu, and sure enough, Kesu read out slowly the letters etched into the beads: "a-w-i'-n-a-k-o-l-a." The children all wondered what it meant.

"awi'nakola means to live as one with nature, land, water, animals, plants and everything on earth," explained the elder. "If you want to discover what it means to live this way, pay attention to every little detail in the world around you. Try to notice every time anything changes. Eventually you will start to learn things, like how your actions affect the animals, plants and water. Our culture comes from the land. Our language comes from the land. Our knowledge comes from the land. The future is on our shoulders, because all living life depends upon each other."

The kids took a moment to process what the elder was saying. After about 10 minutes Kesu said, "That sounds like it will take us a lifetime to learn, but it also sounds like the beginning of a great adventure."

"Are we ready?" asked Bob. "YES, WE ARE," chorused the children and animals.

"Then let's go!" said the littlest girl, who had been silent the whole time.

And together they set out on their next adventure.

The End.

Epilogue

Over time, the kids learned the language. Eventually they started to learn how their actions affect the earth around them, and they encouraged others to do the same.

Years later, when the kids were all grown up, they told (instead of reading) stories to their own children in the native language to keep the language going. The land is cleaner. The water is less polluted. And there is more hope and more believers.

'The First Peoples' Cultural Council has developed resources to sustain and support Indigenous languages, including the First Voices website. To learn more about the Kwakwala language, please visit:

https://www.firstvoices.com/explore/FV/sections/Data/Kwak%27wala/Kwakwala/Kwakwala

about the author

Adelyn "Addy" Sophie Newman-Ting lives in Victoria, British Columbia with her mother, a schoolteacher, and her father, a master carver, professor and First Nations artist. She began to write Finding the Language at age 9 and finished it when she was 10. On her father's side she is Kwakwaka'wakw and Coast Salish, as well as English, Irish and Scottish. On her mother's side, she is Chinese from Taiwan. Her Indigenous name is Kesugilakw meaning leader of people, and her Chinese name is Ting Li-Wen meaning pretty flower cloud. Addy enjoys dancing, baking, jump roping and singing. She is also an avid reader, writer and artist, who loves to spend time with her puppy Harriet. Addy has found the responsibility of being the first Indigenous UNESCO VoFG Child Author, both challenging and rewarding and hopes that this book will raise awareness for the climate, and the importance to saving Indigenous languages and cultures.

about
the
illustrator

Justine Greenfield is an illustrator and oil painter. She studied Art History, and though it still fascinates her, she prefers to create art instead of study it; therefore, she went to the Ontario College of Art and Design (OCAD) University in Toronto, Canada and graduated with a degree in Illustration.

Justine is also a figure skating instructor and loves working with kids. Her work with children and her childhood, which she spent playing in the fields and woods around her home in rural Ontario, serves as the main inspiration for her illustrations. She draws on subject matters that make one chuckle or think to create lovely illustrations suffused with a bit of mystery and fun.

She currently lives and works in Toronto, Canada.

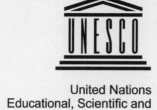

The United Nations Convention on the Rights of the Child

All children are holders of important human rights. Twenty-five years ago in 1989, over a hundred countries agreed on the UN Convention on the Rights of the Child. In the most important human rights treaty in history, they promised to protect and promote all children's equal rights, which are connected and equally important.

In the 54 Articles of the Convention, countries make solemn promises to defend children's needs and dreams. They recognize the role of children in realizing their rights, which requires that children be heard and involved in decision-making. In particular, Article 24 and Article 27 defend children's rights to safe drinking water, good food, a clean and safe environment, health, and quality of life. Article 29 recognizes children's rights to education that develops personality, talents and potential, respecting human rights and the natural environment.

> — *Dr. Alexandra Wandel*
> World Future Council

Sustainable Development Goals Statement

The United Nations Sustainable Development Goals are a bridge from the previous Millennium Development Goals adopted by the international community in 2000 to the future. Construction of this bridge began in 2012 at the United Nations Rio+ 20 Conference on Sustainable Development. At this Conference, countries agreed that it was time to take concrete action for the present and the future by acting on issues such as climate change, poverty, inequality and biodiversity. This resulted in The Future We Want, a global statement of priorities and responsibilities for countries toward the people, environment, biodiversity and future.

In 2015, the bridge took shape in the form of the United Nations Sustainable Development Goals, which countries agreed to implement between 2015 and 2030. The SDGs, as they are commonly called, comprise a set of 17 specific goals, over 160 targets within these goals, and hundreds of indicators to measure if the goals and targets are being met. The SDGs address the key issues that face our world community now and that will define this community in the future, such as poverty, climate change, education rights, gender equality, discrimination, health, food and water access and safety, and the promotion of justice for all members of society. Since 2015, children around the world have joined in efforts to incorporate the SDGs in their countries and communities, adding their voices and perspectives as future leaders. The SDGs show the power of all people, including children, to create positive and lasting change that addresses the needs of local and global society.

— *Dr. Alexandra R. Harrington*
Centre for International Sustainable Development Law

Voices of Future Generations Children's Book Series

Thanks and Inspiring Resources

'Voices of Future Generations' International Commission
Warmest thanks to the International Commission, launched in 2014 by His Excellency Judge CG Weeramantry, UNESCO Peace Education Research Award Laureate, which supports, guides and profiles this new series of Children's Books Series, including:
Ms. Alexandra Wandel (WFC), Prof. Marie-Claire Cordonier Segger (CISDL), Dr Kristiann Allen (New Zealand), Ms. Irina Bokova (Former Director-General UNESCO), Ms. Emma Hopkin / Ms. Hannah Rolls (UK), Ms. Julia Marton-Lefevre (IUCN), Dr James Moody (Australia), Prof. Kirsten Sandberg (UN CRC Chair), Judge Marcel Szabo (Hungary), Dr Christina Voigt (Norway), Dr Alexandra Harrington (CISDL).

'Voices of Future Generations' Goodwill Ambassadors and VoFG Team
Most sincere appreciation to HH Sheikha Hissa Hamdan bin Rashid Al Maktoum (ELF / Middle East), Dr Ying-Shih Hsieh (EQPF / Asia), Dr Gabrielle Sacconaghi-Bacon (Moore Foundation / North America), Ms. Monique Gray Smith (First Nations of Canada), Ms. Melinda Manuel (PNG), Dr Odeeth Lara-Morales (VoFG), Ms. Chiara Rohlfs (VoFG), Ms. Sarah Sanders (VoFG), Ms. Allison Lalla (VoFG), Ms. Hyfa Azzez (VoFG), Neshan Gunasekera (VoFG).

The World Future Council consists of 50 eminent global changemakers from across the globe. Together, they work to pass on a healthy planet and just societies to our children and grandchildren. (www.worldfuturecouncil.org)

United Nations Education, Science and Culture Organization (UNESCO) strives to build networks among nations that enable humanity's moral and intellectual solidarity by mobilizing for education, building intercultural understanding, pursuing scientific cooperation, and protecting freedom of expression. (https://en.unesco.org/)

The **Canadian Commission for UNESCO (CCUNESCO)** serves as a bridge between Canadians and the vital work of UNESCO—the United Nations Educational, Scientific and Cultural Organization. Through its networks and partners, the Commission promotes UNESCO's values, priorities and programs in Canada and brings the voices of Canadian experts to the international stage. The Commission facilitates cooperation and knowledge mobilization in the fields of education, sciences, culture, communication and information to address some of the most complex challenges facing humanity. Its activities are guided by the United Nations' 2030 Agenda for Sustainable Development and other UNESCO priorities. CCUNESCO operates under the authority of the Canada Council for the Arts.

The United Nations Committee on the Rights of the Child (CRC) is the body of 18 independent experts that monitors implementation of the Convention on the Rights of the Child, and its three Optional Protocols, by its State parties. (www.ohchr.org)

United Nations Environment Programme (UNEP) provides leadership and encourages partnership in caring for the environment by inspiring, informing, and enabling nations and peoples to improve their quality of life without compromising that of future generations. (www.unep.org)

International Union for the Conservation of Nature (IUCN) envisions a just world that values and conserves nature, working to conserve the integrity and diversity of nature and to ensure that any use of natural resources is equitable and ecologically sustainable. (www.iucn.org)

Centre for International Sustainable Development Law (CISDL) supports understanding, development and implementation of law for sustainable development by leading legal research through scholarship and dialogue and facilitating legal education through teaching and capacity-building. (www.cisdl.org)

Environmental Quality Protection Foundation (EQPF) established in 1984 is the premier ENGO in Taiwan. Implementing environmental education, tree plantation, and international participation through coordinating transdisciplinary resources to push forward environmental and sustainable development in our time.

World's Largest Lesson (WLL) World's Largest Lesson brings the Global Goals to children all over the world and unites them in taking action. Since it was launched in September 2015, the World's Largest Lesson has reached over 130 countries and impacted over 8 million children each year. (https://worldslargestlesson.globalgoals.org/)

Emirates Literature Foundation, home of the Emirates Airline Festival of Literature is a not-for-profit non-governmental organisation that supports and nurtures a love of literature in the UAE and across the region through a programme of varied cultural initiatives. Recognising the distinctive contribution that literature makes to children's lives, the Foundation focuses on introducing and cultivating a spirit of reading while acting as a catalyst for writing and cultural exchange. (https://www.elfdubai.org/en/home)

About the 'Voices of Future Generations' Series

To celebrate the 25th Anniversary of the United Nations Convention on the Rights of the Child, the Voices of Future Generations Children's Book Series, led by the United Nations and a consortium of educational charities including the World Future Council (WFC), the Centre for International Sustainable Development Law (CISDL), the Environmental Quality Protection Foundation (EQPF), the Fundacion Ecos and the Trust for Sustainable Living (TSL) among others, as well as the Future Generations Commissioners of several countries, and international leaders from the UN Division for Sustainable Development, the UN Committee on the Rights of the Child, the UN Education, Science and Culture Organisation (UNESCO), the International Union for the Conservation of Nature (IUCN), and other international organizations, has launched the new Voices of Future Generations Series of Children's Books.

Every year we feature stories from our selected group of child authors, inspired by the outcomes of the Earth Summit, the Rio+20 United Nations Conference on Sustainable Development (UNCSD) and the world's Sustainable Development Goals, and by the Convention on the Rights of the Child (CRC) itself. Our junior authors, ages 8-12, are concerned about future justice, poverty, the global environment, education and children's rights. Accompanied by illustrations, each book profiles creative, interesting and adventurous ideas for creating a just and greener future, in the context of children's interests and lives.

We aim to publish the books internationally in ten languages, raising the voices of future generations and spread their messages for a fair and sustainable tomorrow among their peers and adults, worldwide. We welcome you to join us in support of this inspiring partnership, at www.vofg.org.

Printed in Great Britain
by Amazon